Hello, Family Members,

Learning to read is one of the most important accomplishments of early childhood. **Hello Reader!** books are designed to help children become skilled readers who like to read. Beginning readers learn to read by remembering frequently used words like "the," "is," and "and"; by using phonics skills to decode new words; and by interpreting picture and text clues. These books provide both the stories children enjoy and the structure they need to read fluently and independently. Here are suggestions for helping your child *before*, *during*, and *after* reading:

Before

- Look at the cover and pictures and have your child predict what the story is about.
- Read the story to your child.
- Encourage your child to chime in with familiar words and phrases.
- Echo read with your child by reading a line first and having your child read it after you do.

During

- Have your child think about a word he or she does not recognize right away. Provide hints such as "Let's see if we know the sounds" and "Have we read other words like this one?"
- Encourage your child to use phonics skills to sound out new words.
- Provide the word for your child when more assistance is needed so that he or she does not struggle and the experience of reading with you is a positive one.
- Encourage your child to have fun by reading with a lot of expression . . . like an actor!

After

- Have your child keep lists of interesting and favorite words.
- Encourage your child to read the books over and over again. Have him or her read to brothers, sisters, grandparents, and even teddy bears. Repeated readings develop confidence in young readers.
- Talk about the stories. Ask and answer questions. Share ideas about the funniest and most interesting characters and events in the stories.

I do hope that you and your child enjoy this book.

— Francie Alexander
Reading Specialist,
Scholastic's Learning Ventures

To Lulu and Maxine

Text copyright © 1999 by Daniel Pinkwater.
Illustrations copyright © 1999 by Jill Pinkwater.
All rights reserved. Published by Scholastic Inc.
SCHOLASTIC, HELLO READER, CARTWHEEL BOOKS and associated logos are trademarks and/or registered trademarks of Scholastic Inc.

Library of Congress Cataloging-in-Publication Data

Pinkwater, Daniel Manus, 1941 -
    Big Bob and the Winter Holiday Potato / by Daniel Pinkwater; illustrated by Jill Pinkwater.
        p.   cm.—(Hello reader! Level 3)
    "Cartwheel Books."
    Summary: For their second-grade class celebration of Kwanzaa, Chanukah, Christmas, and all other winter holidays, Gloria and Big Bob write a play about Potato Claus, friend to children everywhere.
        ISBN 0-439-04243-7 (pb)
        [1. Holidays—Fiction. 2. Theater—Fiction. 3. Potatoes—Fiction.
4. Schools—Fiction.] I. Pinkwater, Jill, ill. II. Title. III. Series.
PZ7.P6335Bw   1999
[E]—dc21   98-49687
                                                                    CIP
                                                                    AC
12 11 10 9 8 7 6 5 4 3 2   01 02 03 04

Printed in the U.S.A.   24
First printing, December 1999

BIG BOB AND THE WINTER HOLIDAY POTATO

by Daniel Pinkwater
Illustrated by Jill Pinkwater

Hello Reader! — Level 3

SCHOLASTIC INC. Cartwheel B·O·O·K·S®

New York Toronto London Auckland Sydney Mexico City New Delhi Hong Kong

Winter Holidays

"It is almost time for the winter holidays," Mr. Salami said.

Mr. Salami is our teacher. He used to be a deep-sea diver, but he got too fat for the suit.

"Winter holidays—Chanukah, Kwanzaa, and Christmas—we will study them all. We will learn different customs. We will have fun."

Big Gloria raised her hand. Big Gloria is my friend. She is the biggest kid in second grade. I am Big Bob. I am the next-biggest after Gloria.

"Will we have a play?" Big Gloria asked.

"I was just coming to that," Mr. Salami said. "We will have a play. Some of us will write the play. Some of us will act in the play. And some of us will watch the play."

"Mr. Salami, I wish to write the play," Big Gloria said.

"Fine. That is fine. You may work on writing the play, Gloria. Who else would like to work on writing the play?"

"Big Bob will help me," Big Gloria said. "Big Bob can help me write the play."

"Good. Bob will help you," said Mr. Salami. "Does anyone else want to write?"

Big Gloria looked around. She looked at all the second graders. No one else wanted to write.

"No one else wants to write," Big Gloria said.

Freedom of Expression

"The play will be about Santa Claus," Mr. Salami said.

"No," Big Gloria said.

"No?" Mr. Salami asked.

"No," Big Gloria said.

"Why no?" Mr. Salami asked.

"Santa Claus is scary," Big Gloria said. "He comes into people's houses at night when they are sleeping. That is scary."

"It is a tradition," Mr. Salami said.

"I don't care," Big Gloria said. "At my house we have a burglar alarm. It rings at the police station. If Santa Claus sneaks into my house, he is going to wind up in jail."

"Everybody loves Santa Claus," Mr. Salami said.

"If I see Santa Claus in my house, I am going to scream," Big Gloria said.

"What would you rather write about?" Mr. Salami asked.

"We will write about Potato Claus," Big Gloria said.

"This play has to be about one of the regular winter holidays," Mr. Salami said. "Is Potato Claus part of any of them?"

"No," Big Gloria said. "I made him up myself."

"Then I can't let you write about him," Mr. Salami said.

"You have to."

"Why?"

"Because if you don't let us write about Potato Claus, you will deny our right to self-expression."

Potato Claus

"What is Potato Claus like and what does he do?" Mr. Salami asked.

"He is nice," Big Gloria said. "He does not sneak into your house at night. He comes in the daytime. He rings the bell. Then he lets children choose their gifts out of a big book. Later, the gifts arrive on a truck from the post office."

"Does Potato Claus ask if you have been a good child or a bad child?" Mr. Salami asked.

"No," Big Gloria said. "He does not get personal like that."

Print Neatly

After school, I went to Big Gloria's house. Big Gloria's mother gave us potato sticks and glasses of milk.

"Let's write the play," Big Gloria said.

"Have you ever written a play before?" I asked.

"No," Big Gloria said, "but I know what to do."

"What?"

"There are two important things about writing a play," Big Gloria said. "First, each time a new person speaks, you put the name of that person at the start of a line, in capital letters."

"What is the other important thing about writing a play?" I asked.

"Print neatly."

We Are Writers

We wrote the play. It was easy. It was fun.

"We are writers!" Big Gloria said.

POPPLETON
IN WINTER